KIDS CAN'T S
THE CHOOSE YOUR
OWN ADVENTURE® STORIES!

"I like Choose Your Own Adventure books because they're full of surprises. I can't wait to read more."

—Cary Romanos, age 12

"Makes you think thoroughly before making decisions."

—Hassan Stevenson, age 11

"I read five different stories in one night and that's a record for me. The different endings are fun."

—Timmy Sullivan, age 9

"It's great fun! I like the idea of making my own decisions."

—Anthony Ziccardi, age 11

And teachers like this series, too:

"We have read and reread, worn thin, loved, loaned, bought for others, and donated to school libraries our Choose Your Own Adventure books."

CHOOSE YOUR OWN ADVENTURE®— AND MAKE READING MORE FUN!

Bantam Books in the Choose Your Own Adventure® Series
Ask your bookseller for the books you have missed

Choose Your Own Adventure Books for younger readers

THE MYSTERY OF URA SENKE

BY SHANNON GILLIGAN

ILLUSTRATED BY PAUL ABRAMS

An R.A. Montgomery Book

BANTAM BOOKS

TORONTO • NEW YORK • LONDON • SYDNEY • AUCKLAND

RL 5, IL age 10 and up

THE MYSTERY OF URA SENKE
A Bantam Book / May 1985

CHOOSE YOUR OWN ADVENTURE® is a registered trademark of
Bantam Books, Inc. Registered in U.S. Patent and Trademark
Office and elsewhere.
Original conception of Edward Packard

ISBN 0-553-24892-8

Published simultaneously in the United States and Canada

Bantam Books are published by Bantam Books, Inc. Its trademark, consisting of the words "Bantam Books" and the por-
trayal of a rooster, is Registered in U.S. Patent and Trademark
Office and in other countries. Marca Registrada. Bantam
Books, Inc., 666 Fifth Avenue, New York, New York 10103.

PRINTED IN THE UNITED STATES OF AMERICA

0   0 9 8 7 6 5 4 3 2 1

WARNING!!!

Do not read this book straight through from beginning to end! These pages contain many different adventures you may have as you search for the priceless tea bowl stolen from Ura Senke. From time to time as you read along, you will be asked to make a choice. Your choice may lead to success or disaster.

The adventures you have will be the result of the decisions you make. *You* are responsible because *you* choose! After you make your choice, follow the instructions to see what happens to you next.

Think carefully before you make a decision. Your detective work might help you find the missing bowl . . . or it might lead you to disaster at the hands of ruthless criminals.

Good luck!

You lie on the couch staring out the window. Another cold gray day. It's January third, the last official day of New Year's celebrations in Japan. Your family is spending the year in Kyoto, and even if Japanese school is three times harder than school in the United States, you'll almost be glad when classes start again in two days. Anything is better than a boring vacation.

Trring, trring, trring—the triple ring of the telephone interrupts your thoughts.

"I'll get it," you yell, jumping up.

"Moshi-moshi," you say into the receiver, answering Japanese-style.

"I'm glad it's you. We need your help."

You recognize the voice of Kenichi Doi, your best friend, on the other end. "What's wrong, Kenichi? Where are you?"

"I can't talk on the phone. I'm at Ura Senke, the tea ceremony school where my older brother, Takashi, studies. Takashi and I are in trouble. Can you meet us here?"

"I'll be there right away," you say.

Turn to page 2.

You tell your mother that you're going out for the rest of the day. Thirty minutes later you walk down a quiet, tree-lined street and approach the main gate to the world-famous Ura Senke School. Kenichi is waiting for you.

"Follow me," he whispers.

You follow your friend along a stone pathway past several buildings. Passing under an archway, you enter a simple, stunning garden and continue toward a small hutlike building at the far end.

"This is the Yu-in Tearoom," Kenichi tells you quietly. "Takashi is inside."

Takashi bows as you crawl in through the low door. "I'm so glad you could come," he says. "Kenichi tells me you solved a mystery once in your own country. I thought that maybe you could help today."

"Mrs. Whepple just had a greedy nephew," you protest. "Figuring out who stole her husband's coin collection was easy. But what's the problem?"

Turn to page 4.

4

Takashi begins, "This morning, just before I was about to perform a tea ceremony for four extremely distinguished guests, I discovered that the tea bowl I had set out to use was missing."

"It was stolen, you mean!" Kenichi says excitedly.

"Yes," Takashi agrees, "I believe it was stolen."

"And it wasn't just a common tea bowl, either," Kenichi adds. "It was a very old and famous bowl, a Shino piece called Yukisoo."

"What's a Shino piece?" you ask.

"Shinoware is a type of pottery that has a mottled white glaze with tinges of gray or red," Takashi explains. "This bowl has grayish blotches near the lip on one side that look like snow clouds; hence the name. *Yukisoo* means 'It looks like snow.' All important tea bowls are eventually named," Takashi adds. "Some are named after a memorable tea ceremony. Others are named for their distinctive appearance—like Yukisoo."

"Several years ago," Kenichi says, "it was made a National Treasure."

"A what?" you ask.

"A National Treasure," Takashi repeats. "It's a work of art—a screen, a painting, or a tea bowl, for instance—so important to the preservation of ancient Japanese culture and tradition that it can never be taken out of the country. All National Treasures are registered at the Ministry of Education up in Tokyo. Their every movement is monitored by someone up at the ministry."

Go on to the next page.

"How much is the bowl worth?" you want to know.

"Hundreds of thousands in U.S. money. Maybe even more on the black market," says Takashi, looking at the floor, "which is where I'm afraid the bowl is headed."

"How long has the bowl been missing?" you ask.

Takashi looks at his watch. "Fifty minutes. The tea ceremony was scheduled for ten-thirty, which is right about the time I noticed that Yukisoo was gone. First I called Kenichi, who then called you. I have searched the garden, the hut, and the waiting alcove thoroughly. The bowl is not anywhere."

Takashi adds after a pause, "I wanted to keep the police out of it as long as possible. A thing like this will make national headlines. It will be a disgrace to the school and a great dishonor to my family."

The first rule of good detective work is to get all the details straight, you think as Takashi finishes speaking. But this job sounds awfully big.

Maybe it's too big?

If you tell Takashi that it's always important to deal with the police on a case like this, turn to page 9.

If you want more information about the four guests and the tea ceremony Takashi planned to perform, turn to page 11.

The woman finally returns to the phone. "I'm sorry," she says, "but there was no one in the Yu-in Tearoom or garden. It was absolutely empty, although Takashi Doi *is* scheduled to be giving a tea in there this morning."

"Thank you," you answer. "I'll try later."

Where could they have gone? Takashi promised he'd stay right there. Something's strange, you think. Even if Takashi *had* gone off for some reason, Kenichi would have stayed.

Ignoring the mysterious black sedan, you run back to Ura Senke. You'd better find out what's going on!

Turn to page 36.

Mr. Hata is staying on the other side of town at the New Miyako Hotel, so the three of you take a cab. When you get there, you walk up to the front desk and ask, "Can you please tell me which room Mr. Shoji Hata is using?"

The clerk checks his files. "Mr. Hata checked out a few minutes ago," he answers.

"Did he say where he was going?" Takashi asks.

"No, but why don't you ask the doorman who got him a cab? He might know the direction he was headed."

Turn to page 21.

"Takashi, the police will be a big help on a job like this. Besides, I'm sure they'll keep the news quiet if you ask them," you say.

Takashi thinks for a moment, then shrugs his shoulders. "I suppose you're right. But will you go get them? I don't want to use the office phone yet, and it will draw less suspicion if you go for help instead of me."

"Sure," you agree. You say good-bye to Takashi and Kenichi, find your way back out to the school's gate, and head toward the police box located a few blocks away. The street is quiet except for the black sedan driving slowly along a half block behind you.

Why is it going so slowly? you wonder. When you look back, you see that the car is getting closer. An eerie feeling creeps over you, and your palms begin to sweat. Are you being followed? Two men are sitting in the front seat, and they seem to be looking straight at you.

If you break into a run, turn to page 15.

If you walk up to the phone booth on the corner and pretend to make a call while you get a better look at the black car, turn to page 20.

When you wake up, your head throbs and you feel woozy. You're sitting tied to a chair in someone's library. Books line the walls from floor to ceiling. Outside you hear the lapping of waves against a shore. Two people are talking in the next room.

Are you at the seashore? Or maybe Lake Biwa outside of Kyoto? Suddenly the two voices get louder. They're having some kind of argument, but you can't make out what they're saying. Then it's quiet again, and you hear the sound of a phone being dialed.

"Hello. May I speak to Mrs. Oda, please?" a gruff male voice barks. After a pause, he continues, "Mrs. Oda? Yosuimoto here. Yukio-chan's boss."

"I know you've finished taking care of your son's debts, Mrs. Oda. But there's a reason you might reconsider that position," the voice says after a pause.

"What kind of reason? The Shino bowl, Mrs. Oda. We have it. Mr. Hata is on his way to Germany with a fake, I'm afraid. Is the Shino bowl a good enough reason?"

So *they've* got the missing tea bowl, you tell yourself. And whoever this Mrs. Oda is wants it too.

"Good, Mrs. Oda," the voice continues, "I knew you would be reasonable. Bring fifty million yen out to our location on Lake Biwa. Come alone. I will notify my man at the gate to let you through."

Turn to page 18.

"Who were the guests, Takashi?" you ask.

"There were four altogether," Takashi answers. "Noriko Oda, Taro Sakamoto, Hiro Narita, and Shoji Hata."

"Taro Sakamoto?" you ask. The name rings a bell. "Doesn't he have a good chance of being elected Prime Minister this spring?"

"Yes," Takashi replies, "but only if Mr. Narita and his followers in the Japanese congress do not oppose him. Mrs. Oda, a gem trader here in Kyoto, is a friend of both men. She felt that a tea ceremony at New Year's would be a good place for them to, as you Americans say, bury the hatchet."

"Where does Shoji Hara come in?" you ask

"Hata," Takashi says, correcting you. "Mr. Hata is an official from the Ministry of Arts. He is an old friend of Mrs. Oda's as well. A few days ago Mrs. Oda asked if he might be invited to the tea. In the meantime an official request came from the Ministry of Arts that several National Treasures owned by the school, including Yukisoo, be used during the tea ceremony so Mr. Hata could inspect them."

"What happens at a tea ceremony?" you ask.

"Basically you serve tea," Takashi replies. "But you do so within a strict framework of prescribed actions that has evolved over hundreds of years. There is a standard way of performing each step, of making each movement, during a tea ceremony—from greeting your guests to whisking the tea itself."

Go on to the next page.

"I don't get it," you say. "What's so interesting about it, then?"

Suddenly Takashi, who has seemed somewhat tense and formal, loosens up. "Why, *everything* is interesting," he says. "The choice of utensils, how they reflect the weather and season, the mood of the guests and the host, how carefully the ritual of performing tea is adhered to, how it is departed from." Takashi nods and smiles. "Yes, *everything* about tea is interesting."

"Do students of the tea ceremony like yourself often perform the ceremony for such important guests?" you ask.

"Not usually," Takashi replies, "but Mrs. Oda is an old patron of Ura Senke. She is particularly supportive of us younger ones studying tea. All she asked my teacher, Kitamuki-sensei, was that the ceremony be performed by one of his more talented students."

"One day Takashi will be the greatest tea master in Japan," Kenichi adds proudly.

"Not if I don't recover the Shino piece," Takashi snaps.

"Tell me, Takashi," you say, "do you know any of the guests personally? Is there anything unusual about them?"

Go on to the next page.

"Mrs. Oda I see from time to time around the school. She is always cordial enough. I know she travels abroad frequently to buy and sell gems. I also knew her son years ago when we were together in junior high. But later he fell into gambling and drinking and finally dropped out of school. I know nothing about the politicians except what you read in the papers. And today was the first time I met Mr. Hata, although several people at the school have mentioned him before."

You stroke your chin in thought. "I think I'd like to talk to each of the guests individually."

If you'd like to talk first to Taro Sakamoto, the man who wants to be Prime Minister, go on to the next page.

If you'd like to talk first to Shoji Hata, from the Ministry of Arts, turn to page 7.

If you'd like to talk first to Noriko Oda, the gem dealer, turn to page 25.

If you'd like to talk first to Hiro Narita, Mr. Sakamoto's rival, turn to page 28.

14

Taro Sakamoto is staying at the famous Hiragayama Ryokan, a traditional Japanese-style inn in downtown Kyoto. You, Kenichi, and Takashi go there and are greeted by a kind old woman in the entryway. "Mr. Sakamoto left early this morning at about a quarter to ten. He won't be returning until one-thirty," she tells you. "May I tell him you called?"

"No, no, thank you," Takashi says, bowing. "We will try to return later today."

You and Kenichi bow as well and follow Takashi out onto the street.

"Now where?" Kenichi asks.

*If you decide to go to Noriko Oda's next,
turn to page 25.*

*If you decide to go to Shoji Hata's next,
turn to page 7.*

*If you decide to go to Hiro Narita's next,
turn to page 28.*

You start to run, and the black car speeds up behind you. It pulls right up onto the sidewalk, forcing you to stop. The man in the front seat flings his door open and leaps out.

"What do you think you're—" you start to say. But before you can finish, the man grabs you by the shoulder, pressing a nerve. You crumple to the sidewalk, motionless.

Go on to the next page.

A short while later you begin to wake up. You're in the black car, and the two men are driving you somewhere. Seeing you move, one of them pulls a syringe from the glove compartment and jabs it into your arm. "You won't be able to help your friends find the tea bowl now!" he cackles.

You are too weak to defend yourself. But before

the drug takes effect, you notice the elaborate, grotesque tattoos peeping above the collars on each man's neck. It's the sign of the Yakuza—the treacherous Japanese Mafia—you realize, before you pass out again.

Turn to page 10.

Fifty million yen! That's over two hundred thousand dollars! Takashi wasn't kidding when he said the bowl was worth a lot. You've *got* to escape and get hold of it before Mrs. Oda does.

You hear the people in the next room leave. You're still tied to the chair, but the ropes are loose. You remember from a movie you once saw that if you stand up and wiggle continuously, the ropes should loosen enough so that you can free yourself.

It works! In a few minutes you are padding quietly around the room, trying to decide the best escape route. There's the door, but who knows what's beyond? You were unconscious when they brought you in, and you don't remember anything about the rest of the house.

The only other way out would be by the window. You look out at the winter remnants of a vegetable garden. At least no one should be hanging around gardening at this time of year, you think. And a thick grove of pine trees is at the other end. Maybe you could escape through those woods.

If you decide to try the door, turn to page 22.

If you decide to climb out through the window, turn to page 26.

When you get to the phone booth and begin dialing, the black car stops and sits idling by the curb. The operator comes over the wire. "What number would you like?" she says in a polite voice.

"Ura Senke, the tea school," you blurt out, not thinking. Mechanically you dial the number she gives you, and a woman answers, "Ura Senke Tea School."

"Hello, may I speak to Takashi Doi? He's out in the Yu-in Tearoom."

"Just a moment," she responds. "I'll go get him."

The minutes tick by. It seems as if it's taking her forever. The black car doesn't move.

Turn to page 6.

"A short, studious-looking man with glasses, you say?" the doorman asks, scratching his head.

"Yes. He left only fifteen minutes ago," you reply.

"I know which one you mean," the doorman says. "I noticed him for two reasons. First he was carrying a wooden box, wrapped in an expensive purple silk scarf, that he wouldn't so much as let me touch. Second I heard him direct the cab driver to Kobe Seaport, Dock Number Nineteen. Not too many cruise ships out of Kobe this time of year, are there?"

You thank the doorman, trying to hide your excitement.

"Well, *this* is an interesting turn," you say to your friends.

"Yes," Takashi agrees, "but I don't have time to go all the way to Kobe. I have to return and tell my teacher that the bowl is gone. I hope that won't stop you two."

"No chance," Kenichi says enthusiastically. "Which way should we go? By express train or taxi? It's a holiday, so traffic will be thin. The cab will probably be faster. On the other hand an express train will be much cheaper."

If you go by train, turn to page 33.

If you go by taxi, turn to page 29.

You walk over to the door and listen. Heavy rhythmic snores punctuate the quiet. Whoever is supposed to be guarding you has fallen asleep.

Opening the door, you carefully step over the sleeping figure curled in front of it. His jacket lies partly open, exposing a gun in a holster jutting out from his hip. That gun could be just what you need to get out of here!

Just then the snoring guard starts to stir.

If you try to grab the gun and run off up the hall, turn to page 39.

If you think it's too risky to steal the gun, and decide to take off before the guard awakes, turn to page 44.

Mrs. Oda's is within walking distance, so the three of you set off. Ten minutes later you ring the bell at her front gate. An ancient servant answers, and you step forward. "We are friends of Mrs. Oda's from Ura Senke and would like to talk to her. Is she in?" you ask.

The servant nods curtly and snaps, "Follow me." He disappears abruptly, and the three of you hurry after as he leads you through Mrs. Oda's exquisite front garden and around to the side.

"I knew Mrs. Oda was rich," says Kenichi, staring around in wonder, "but not this rich."

There's a small fish pond off to one corner with a bucket of bloody red meat next to it. Noticing your surprised look, the servant explains, "When you rang, I was feeding Mrs. Oda's pet fish."

"Fish?" you ask.

"Piranha," the old man says, smiling as he motions you to sit in a small front parlor. "I will tell Mrs. Oda you are here."

"Some pet," you mutter as the servant slides the door shut. But before Takashi or Kenichi can say anything, there is a click as the door slides back and Mrs. Oda steps through. She is a short plump woman with heavy jowls and curiously old-fashioned glasses. She is wearing an expensive silk kimono, and a large diamond flashes on her right pinkie.

"Why, Takashi," she exclaims, "what a pleasant surprise! I hope you bring news of the missing tea bowl?"

Turn to page 27.

You tiptoe to the window and yank the latch. But instead of the window, a portion of the bookshelf suddenly swings open. There's a staircase behind it leading down to an unlit hallway. Maybe it's another way out!

Carefully you descend the stairs, trying to be as quiet as possible. At first you can't see anything, but as your eyes get accustomed to the dark you can make out a door on one wall. The hallway continues another twenty feet before veering to the left.

If you follow the hallway till the end, turn to page 46.

If you try the door instead, turn to page 51.

"No," Takashi replies, bowing, "unfortunately I don't. But I would like—"

Before Takashi finishes speaking, Mrs. Oda interrupts. "Well, no matter. Since you are here anyway, I insist on your staying for a cup of tea. And perhaps you might like to examine my tearoom? It's rather small, but most find it interesting nonetheless. I bought it years and years ago from an old temple on the outskirts of the city. It was before the prices of those things went way up. I had it taken apart and . . ."

You're beginning to think that Mrs. Oda is going to go on in this way nonstop when she's called away to the phone. She returns in about ten minutes. But now her manner has changed completely.

Turn to page 32.

Hiro Narita lives out near Arashiyama, a picturesque part of Kyoto popular with tourists. The streets leading up to his house are filled with people in gaily colored kimonos still celebrating the holiday. Mr. Narita answers the doorbell himself. He invites the three of you in for *zenzai,* a sweet soup made with soybeans and pounded rice cakes served only at New Year's.

"We are honored by your kind invitation, Mr. Narita," Takashi says politely, "but my brother's friend is helping us search for the missing tea bowl, and we only wanted to ask you a few questions. I am afraid we don't have much time."

"Ah, yes. A valuable piece, that Yukisoo," Mr. Narita says thoughtfully. "If you want to know my opinion," he adds, "I wouldn't put it past Mr. Sakamoto to have arranged to have the bowl 'disappear' for a few hours. That way the tea ceremony could be postponed, and he will be saved the shame of having to patch up our old political quarrels. A proud man, that Sakamoto."

Turn to page 30.

You say good-bye to Takashi, promising to call him at Ura Senke if you discover anything. After giving your cab driver directions to Kobe, you settle back in your seats to doze.

Halfway there, you are rudely shaken from sleep when your cab is sideswiped by a hit-and-run driver. The car is badly damaged. You're dazed, but all right.

The driver turns to you. "I could have sworn that that car was waiting at the intersection for us! Then they didn't even stop!"

You look over at Kenichi. He's grimacing in pain.

"Kenichi, what's wrong?" you ask.

"My arm," he says weakly.

It's then that you see the deep gash in Kenichi's left arm surrounded by a quickly spreading bloodstain.

"We've got to get you to the hospital!" you exclaim.

Later that afternoon, while you wait in a nearby hospital emergency room for Kenichi to get stitches, you remember the cab driver's comments. "I could have sworn that that car was waiting . . ."

Maybe someone heard you ask for Mr. Hata at the hotel and followed you? A shiver of fear travels down your back. For now you're *glad* that your search for the missing Shino piece has come to a halt.

The End

30

Mr. Narita's manner is smooth and oily—like a typical politician, you think. It's typical, too, that he's suspicious of his rival Mr. Sakamoto. But something about him tells you he had nothing to do with the theft of the bowl.

"Thank you, Mr. Narita," you say. "Your idea is worth looking into. We'll call on Mr. Sakamoto immediately."

Smiling smugly at your praise, he bows and lets the three of you out.

"I think he's a little paranoid," you tell your friends as you walk back to the train station, "but let's give his theory a try and go question Mr. Sakamoto."

Turn to page 34.

"Takashi, you must excuse me"—Mrs. Oda laughs icily—"but a problem has just arisen that requires my immediate attention. I hate to ask you to leave so soon. Another time, perhaps, you might like to come and see the tearoom."

"Of course," Takashi says, standing and bowing politely. You and Kenichi follow. As soon as you are back out on the street, Kenichi says, "Boy, did she ever switch from hot to cold! I wonder what that phone call was all about."

"I know," you agree. "Something felt awfully suspicious. I'd certainly like to know more about her."

"I have a friend who works for her gem business. Maybe you'd like to talk to him," Takashi suggests.

"But," Kenichi says, trying to peek back into Mrs. Oda's garden through a crack in the gate, "something tells me it might be worthwhile to stake this place out for a while and watch where Mrs. Oda goes."

If you decide to interview Takashi's friend, turn to page 40.

If you decide to keep watch at Mrs. Oda's to see if she goes anywhere, turn to page 37.

"We'll be in touch with you the minute we discover anything," you promise Takashi as he leaves for Ura Senke. You and Kenichi head for the train station in the basement of the Takashimaya Department Store. You jump on a *tokkyuu,* or super-express, bound for Osaka. An hour later in Osaka, you stop to buy a newspaper before switching trains for Kobe.

"Why'd you buy the paper?" Kenichi asks.

"To check on boat departures from Kobe," you reply, turning toward the schedule printed in the back. "Here we are. Dock Nineteen. The *Crane of Happiness* leaves for Germany at three thirty. We'll be just in time."

Turn to page 60.

A half hour later Mr. Sakamoto is pouring tea for you in his chambers at the Hiragayama Ryokan, an inn in downtown Kyoto.

Mr. Sakamoto laughs. "Typical of Mr. Narita to think I stole the tea bowl to prevent a reconciliation. Why would I do that when a reconciliation can only benefit me?"

You try a different tack. "Is there anything at all, Mr. Sakamoto, that you noticed was odd or unusual at Ura Senke while you were waiting for the tea ceremony to begin?" you ask.

"Well, I didn't mention it at the time. I felt it would be inappropriate and that it might insult Takashi's mastery of tea," Sakamoto answers, bowing briefly to Takashi, "but at the same moment that Takashi walked out into the garden to welcome us, I noticed a maid—or someone dressed like a maid—dart through a back gate beyond the tea hut. No one else could have seen her, especially Takashi. He was on the other side of the hut welcoming us. I assumed she had brought some forgotten item at the last minute or some hot food to be served."

"There was no maid in or near the tea hut all morning!" Takashi exclaims. "She must be the one who took the bowl."

Go on to the next page.

"Well, it certainly narrows down the suspects," you agree.

You thank Mr. Sakamoto for his help and hurry back to Ura Senke to find out which maids were on duty that day.

The housekeeper tells you that only one of the maids, Akiko Tanaka, was working that morning.

"She lives with her grandparents in a farming community an hour outside of Kyoto," the house-keeper continues, "but I know she moonlights as a bar hostess at a place called the Blue Rabbit down-town."

You discover that the Blue Rabbit is only fifteen minutes away by taxi, but it will take you considerably longer to get out to Akiko Tanaka's house. The more time that passes after a crime, the less chance you have of solving it, you think. What should you do?

If you decide to go to the Blue Rabbit first, turn to page 84.

If you decide to go directly to Akiko's house, turn to page 94.

You head toward the tea school gate, but before you get there, Takashi and Kenichi come running up to you.

"I'm so glad we caught you in time!" Takashi gasps. "Kenichi has had a brilliant idea."

You turn to Kenichi, who says, "Before we do anything else, we should go ask Mrs. Hamaguchi from Kamigamo Shrine about the Shino bowl. Her powers are truly marvelous."

"Who's Mrs. Hamaguchi?" you ask.

"She's one of the best fortune-tellers in all of Japan. She'll be able to tell us where the bowl is. Come on!" Kenichi replies.

Your friends tear off, and there's nothing you can do but follow.

But a fortune-teller? you wonder.

Turn to page 71.

You position yourselves up the street, where you can't be seen from Mrs. Oda's, and settle in for a wait. Mrs. Oda doesn't disappoint you. Forty-five minutes later her servant unbolts the heavy side doors to her property and drives a shiny new black Toyota around to the front. Mrs. Oda emerges from the front gate wearing a navy-blue Western-style suit. She says something to the old man and gets into the driver's seat. The servant disappears inside.

"Did you hear what she was saying?" Takashi asks.

"No," you respond, "but let's follow her. Kenichi, run out to Horikawa Street and get a cab. Takashi and I will stay here and watch which way she turns."

Turn to page 42.

You dart forward quickly and slip the revolver from its holster. The guard turns over. For a moment you are paralyzed by the fear that he might be waking up, but in a few seconds his snoring resumes. You tiptoe up the edge of the hallway, where the wood is least likely to creak. Suddenly you hear voices from around the corner. You have no choice but to duck behind the door immediately in front of you.

You find yourself in a room that looks like a storage area for art works. Scrolls are rolled up and wrapped in their silk coverings. A large antique *sake* urn sits in a wooden crate in the center of the room, partially packed. Boxes holding vases, incense burners, and tea bowls are neatly stacked on shelves along one wall. You wonder if one of them contains the Shino bowl, but you don't have the chance to check. The voices round the corner and come closer.

You have to hide, but there's no closet! Where can you go?

Turn to page 43.

Luckily Takashi's friend Jiro is at home, and he is more than willing to talk about his employer.

"Mrs. Oda is an extremely private person. As far as I can tell, she's close to none of her fifty or so employees. She's an excellent businesswoman—cool, tough, some say ruthless. In the gem business you have to be. It's a world full of petty rivalries and jealousies, even an occasional murder."

Jiro takes a drag on a cigarette and continues. "I don't know why Mrs. Oda might have stolen the Shino bowl. She's quite wealthy. She could probably afford a bowl of similar value already on the market."

"Have you noticed anything peculiar around the office lately, anything out of the ordinary?" you ask. "Not necessarily having to do with Mrs. Oda personally."

"As a matter of fact, I have," Jiro replies. "I'm in the accounting department, as you know. Well, earlier this past week we received a check from someone in Germany for three hundred thousand dollars. That's a large amount, even for Mrs. Oda's business, so I thought I'd better look into it. The letter that came with it merely indicated that it was for 'goods ordered.' When I checked with the jewelers, there wasn't a piece of that value being made. Nor was there an order in for it. I was planning to ask Mrs. Oda herself about it this coming week."

Go on to the next page.

"Do you remember the name of the person who wrote the check?" you ask Jiro.

"No, but I've got a key to the office," he replies. "Let's go down and check. Now you've got *me* interested."

Turn to page 50.

Kenichi returns with a cab a few minutes later.

"We're following a black Toyota," you tell the cab driver, climbing in. "It took a left at the next corner up ahead. Step on it, please."

The cab driver follows Mrs. Oda's route, but back out on Horikawa Street you don't see the black sedan anywhere.

"Over there!" Kenichi suddenly shouts, pointing, just as the black car takes a left and heads downtown. "She must be going toward her shop."

Sure enough, a short while later Mrs. Oda pulls into an alley alongside an impressive building with a black marble front. ODA GEMS, say the elegant characters cut into the stone over the display window. You let the cab go and crouch behind a car parked opposite the alleyway. Mrs. Oda unlocks a side entrance and disappears inside.

"Now is my chance," you whisper to Takashi and Kenichi. "I'm going to hide in her trunk and go along for the ride."

"Don't you think that's a bit risky?" Takashi asks. "If she discovers you, who knows what she'll do? I say we wait to see what she does."

If you decide to wait, turn to page 47.

If you tell Takashi that you'll be safe, and then get into the trunk quickly before Mrs. Oda returns, turn to page 49.

Suddenly you have an idea. Lifting up the lid of the large *sake* urn, you climb inside. You pull the lid back on just as the men you heard open the door and walk into the room—right over to the jar you're hidden in. You can hear them packing paper tightly between the urn and the sides of the crate. Then they put the crate lid on and nail it into place.

Turn to page 54.

The guard just turns over and continues to snore. You breathe a sigh of relief. But as you tip-toe quickly up the hallway the stillness is suddenly broken by a loud *crrk*! What bad luck! You've stepped on a squeaky board.

The guard jerks awake. You try to run, but he's seen you. He shouts, "The foreigner has escaped. Help!"

As soon as he yells, several more gun-toting henchmen appear from nowhere. One of them is from the car that kidnapped you.

"This time, kid, my shot's going to knock you out for good," he says.

The End

The hallway is long, dark, and damp. At the far end you come to a set of steps leading to an overhead hatch. It must be some kind of secret escape!

You push against the hatch as hard as you can. Finally it gives, and you find yourself in a boathouse at the lake's edge.

It's empty except for an old rowboat and a large dove-gray motorboat tied up to two of the slips. A closer look tells you that the motorboat *does* have its keys. But the rowboat won't make any noise when you leave—it might be the safer means of escape.

Either way you'll be well-hidden once you're thirty feet from shore. The famous Lake Biwa fog is rolling in.

*If you decide to leave by motorboat,
turn to page 62.*

*If you decide to use the rowboat to escape,
turn to page 58.*

You look at Takashi's and Kenichi's faces and realize that they're enjoying this chase as much as you.

"Okay," you say with a smile and a shrug, "let's stick together."

Just then Mrs. Oda reemerges from the side door.

"Look," you exclaim, "she's got something heavy inside that leather purse she's carrying. I bet it's the tea bowl!"

You leap up and run toward Mrs. Oda. "What have you got in that purse?" you yell.

"Stop!" Kenichi and Takashi shout, running after you. "Stop!"

Mrs. Oda looks up in shock as the three of you run toward her, and clutches her purse tightly to her chest. You are caught by surprise when she suddenly swings her arm out.

Whomp! She sends you flying through the air with a strong left hook. Your head cracks against the pavement as you land.

Ignoring Mrs. Oda, Kenichi and Takashi crouch with worried looks beside your unconscious figure. They don't even notice her as she drives away, tossing an evil and triumphant grin in your direction.

The End

"Meet me back at Ura Senke. If I don't show up by five tonight, call the police," you tell Takashi and Kenichi before you dash across the street to Mrs. Oda's car. Luckily the trunk is unlocked. You hop in, pulling it shut after you, but making sure it doesn't catch.

A few minutes later you hear the front car door open. A key turns in the ignition. As you head off, an occasional peek out the back tells you that you're heading out of Kyoto.

An hour later Mrs. Oda turns off at the exit for Lake Biwa. She begins driving more slowly and eventually stops. Through the trunk you can hear muffled voices, then the electric whir of some kind of gate. The car ascends a long driveway through a wooded glen.

Talk about expensive properties! you think, peeking out. Mrs. Oda's large garden is nothing compared to this place. A rich green lawn spotted with white birch extends as far as you can see in either direction. Finally the car comes to a stop and Mrs. Oda gets out. There are several people around—you can tell by the crunch of gravel under their feet. Then they walk away and it's silent.

If you get out of the trunk to take a look around, turn to page 65.

If you wait in the car a few more minutes to make sure the coast is really clear, turn to page 59.

The four of you get into a cab and head to Jiro's office. He lets you in through a side door to the building and goes directly to a file cabinet, where he starts flipping through letters.

After a few minutes he says, "Here it is. The name is Schomberg. *Herr* Hugo Schomberg."

"Hugo Schomberg! He's a famous teaware collector from Munich," Takashi exclaims. "He's building a museum for it or something. Mrs. Oda must be stealing the Shino piece for him."

"Get a photocopy of the letter," you direct Jiro. "We're going to the police."

Just then the outside door opens and shuts. Footsteps approach the office where you stand.

"Hide!" Jiro whispers fiercely.

If you hide under a desk, turn to page 56.

If you jump into the closet, turn to page 55.

The door opens with a shove. You flick on the light switch. It illuminates a large room filled with some bulky machinery covered by a tarp.

You lift up the edge to see what's underneath. It's an elaborate four-color printing press. You flick open one of the boxes next to it. Neatly stacked inside are piles of ten-thousand-yen notes.

First it was the tea bowl. Now it's a counterfeiting operation as well! If you can solve these two crimes, your reputation as a detective will be made!

As you stand daydreaming about your achievements, you're jerked back to attention by sudden, sharp popping sounds. It's machine-gun fire, muffled through the walls of the house. Someone outdoors is talking through a bullhorn, but you can't understand what he's saying. Then you hear people in the library above. They're coming down!

Turn to page 69.

You and Kenichi are among the last persons to leave the *Crane of Happiness* before it pulls out to sea. The cab ride back to Kyoto is quiet. Neither of you talks much. As you approach the city limits Kenichi says, "I hate to return to Ura Senke empty-handed. Let's try to finish interviewing the other guests."

"I agree with you. Let's go meet Mrs. Oda. She's the one who organized the whole tea ceremony to begin with," you suggest.

Turn to page 100.

Then Kenichi darts forward! He runs up to hug you, exclaiming, "It's the truth!"

"The men you want are in a room down there," you say, pointing to the stairs. "I locked them into their hiding place behind some boxes."

The policemen dash off, and you turn to Kenichi. "How did you find me?"

"We saw you get kidnapped by the two men in that black car near Ura Senke. I grabbed a policeman, and we managed to follow you out here. The police have been trying to pinpoint the location of this Yakuza operation for months. They were planning a raid anyway. Your kidnap was the straw that broke the camel's back."

"I heard them talking. They've got the Shino bowl," you tell your friend, "and they were planning to sell it to Mrs. Oda."

"I know," Kenichi answers. "They caught her outside a few minutes ago. She's confessed to the whole thing. But unfortunately what they were trying to sell her was a fake."

"You mean the real bowl is still missing?" you ask.

"Yup," Kenichi says, smiling. "The search for the missing Shino piece has only just begun."

The End

"This thing is heavier than I remember it," one of them grunts, hoisting the crate up.

"Where is the boss selling it?" his friend asks.

"To a dealer in Italy. It's leaving by plane from Osaka tonight," you hear him respond.

You shiver. Unless you can figure a safe way out of the urn before the plane departs, you're in for a long, cold flight.

The End

You jump into the closet. Kenichi follows. You close the door just as the other door opens and the footsteps enter. Your heart beats loudly as the footsteps move nearer. Suddenly the door to the closet opens—and Mrs. Oda stares you in the face.

Not knowing what else to do, you jump out at her. "You stole the Shino bowl, and we've got proof!" you shout.

"But," she says, smiling cruelly, "if I destroy you *and* the proof, how will anyone ever find out?"

She pulls out a small gun and fires, but you don't hear the shots. The last thing you notice as you crumple to the ground is that Mrs. Oda has used a silencer.

The End

Takashi, Kenichi, and Jiro have the same impulse as you. All four of you dive underneath desks just seconds before the office door swings open . . . and Mrs. Oda enters!

She walks over to the coat closet and pulls out a large leather purse. Then, heading for a large painting, she presses a secret catch in the frame. The painting swings back to reveal a small safe. Moving quickly, she opens the safe and pulls out twelve thick stacks of bills, which she puts in her purse. Then she closes up the safe, zips the bag, and leaves the office.

Jiro jumps up and asks, "What did she do? I couldn't see from where I was hiding."

"She took a lot of money from a safe hidden behind that painting and left," you tell him.

"We've got to stop her! Suppose she's going to try to leave the country with the Shino piece?" Kenichi asks.

Turn to page 68.

You slip the oars of the rowboat into the water soundlessly. No one seems to notice you go. In a short while you're completely hidden by the fog. You begin rowing more vigorously.

By the time you notice the water slowly filling the bottom of the boat, you are well out on the open lake. You try turning back in, but a strong current carries you out again. Your only chance of survival is to try swimming in. But as soon as you hit the water, you realize that at these icy temperatures, you have a few more minutes to live at best.

The End

You decide you'd better wait here a few more minutes, just to be safe. You don't hear anything else, and you're about to get out of the trunk when two shots are fired close by. Several people run back and forth past the car shouting, but you can't understand much of what they're saying.

"I don't know what's going on, but I sure will be glad to get out of here," you say quietly to yourself as Mrs. Oda gets into the driver's seat and starts the engine. A few seconds later the whole car starts to jiggle violently as if you were driving over a washboard. But when you open the trunk and stick your head out, you see it's no washboard. The car races along a wooden dock, picking up speed. A man you don't recognize jumps out of the driver's seat just before the car dives straight into Lake Biwa.

Turn to page 97.

When you arrive at Kobe Seaport, you head straight for Gate Number 19. "Has Mr. Shoji Hata boarded yet?" you ask an official.

"I wouldn't know," the man replies. "Why don't you check with the steward in the Bon Voyage Lounge? Passengers are loading right now."

You run up three flights of stairs to the Bon Voyage room, where friends and relatives can say good-bye to travelers. A lone figure in the corner leans against the railing, gazing out to sea. A box wrapped in a purple silk scarf sits on the chair next to him.

"Most honorable Mr. Hata!" you call out. Hata glances up and takes one look before grabbing the box and darting through a door that leads into the ship itself. No officials are looking, so you follow him. He disappears down the end of the hallway.

"Let's go after him," you tell Kenichi, starting up the hall.

"Wait!" Kenichi yells after you. "Why don't we get him at his cabin? He has to return there eventually. Besides, we don't know our way around this boat at all."

Go on to the next page.

If you chase after Mr. Hata, turn to page 76.

If you go find out Mr. Hata's cabin number and wait for him there, turn to page 70.

Making as little noise as possible, you untie the motorboat from its pier and shove off. You turn the ignition key, and the engine turns over. Then it noisily sputters out. Oh, no! You turn the key again, and the same thing happens. Now they've noticed you up at the house. Someone yells, "The foreigner is getting away in the boat!"

Three men with revolvers dash across the lawn.

A bullet whistles past you, and you gulp. But you can't let your fear slow you down. You pull out the choke and try starting the boat one more time. *Vrrrooom!* It purrs to life. Just before the first rifle shot is fired from the roof of the house, you slam the boat into forward and disappear into the mist.

Go on to the next page.

As soon as you're safely out of range, you realize you don't know the first thing about Lake Biwa's layout. And it's not helping that you can't see farther than fifty feet ahead because of the fog. Forty minutes later you've used up half a tank of gas—and you still haven't spotted a shoreline. The fog drifts clammily around you. You keep hearing eerie splashes from invisible birds. Your fingers and toes are getting numb from the cold. Nervously you eye the gas gauge. If your luck doesn't change, you're not going to last very long.

Turn to page 75.

You open the trunk a crack. If anyone sees you, they'll investigate—but the coast is clear. You dive into some bushes nearby and begin circling the large, elegant house.

You can hear voices coming through one of the windows and stop to listen. But before you hear anything else, two shots are fired inside the room. They're so close to your head that your ears ring.

A door inside slides open. "Help me take her away," an invisible man orders. You peek over the window ledge just in time to see Mrs. Oda's plump body being dragged from the room by two men wearing dark suits and sunglasses. The room is empty except for a small white ceramic bowl sitting next to its box on a low table.

The Shino piece!

Turn to page 83.

"Let's stay," you say to Kenichi. "If Mr. Hata does have the Shino piece and gets away now, we'll never get it back."

You wait in Mr. Hata's cabin for the rest of the afternoon. But Mr. Hata never returns. Late that evening you realize that he must have gotten back off the ship before it left port.

You and Kenichi can't hide forever. A few days later a steward discovers the two stowaways on board. But instead of sending you back to Kobe, the ship's staff makes you wash pots all the way to the next stop—Hong Kong.

The End

"I know what to do," Jiro says confidently.

Running over to a desk on the other side of the room, he opens a drawer and presses a button. Instantly the air is filled with the shriek of an ear-splitting burglar alarm. Seconds later Mrs. Oda bursts back inside the office. This time you're ready for her. You and Takashi pin her to the ground while Kenichi dials the police.

"What are you doing?" Mrs. Oda screams. "Get off me, you animals!"

"HOLD EVERYTHING!" booms a loud voice.

You whip around to see Jiro pointing a gun into Kenichi's back. "Stop dialing," he barks. "And you two get off her now!"

You and Takashi are so surprised that you obey automatically.

"Good work, Jiro," says Mrs. Oda, standing up and smiling maliciously at the three of you.

"Why, you're in this together!" you gasp.

"Of course," says Jiro. "What did you think? That Mrs. Oda gives every lowly accountant a key to the office? You're a good detective, my friend, but not good enough.

"Not to worry, though," Jiro adds, chuckling. "Your career is about to come to an end anyway."

The End

You turn off the lights and duck under the tarp just before several men dash into the room. They lock the door after themselves and begin moving boxes around. Peeking out, you see that they're uncovering a trap door.

"They'll never find us here!" one of them says, chuckling.

"Don't be so sure," another answers roughly. "Come on."

The last man to disappear pulls the boxes back into place and shuts the small square door with a thud.

The room is suddenly quiet. You steal out from under the tarp and carefully peer over a stack of boxes at their hiding place. The trap door would be impossible to spot if you weren't looking for it. A small latch in the floor is the only sign of anything unusual.

It's time to leave. Maybe there's a way out up the hallway. But as you're leaving the room you spy a rusty padlock on a hook above the light switch.

You smile to yourself. First things first!

Turn to page 93.

You find out from the second mate that Mr. Hata is booked into Cabin Number 111. When you find it, the door is unlocked, and no one's inside. A steamer trunk and suitcase sit at the foot of the narrow bed.

"At least his luggage is here," Kenichi says, "so he should be returning sooner or later."

As Kenichi speaks you notice the red message light on Mr. Hata's phone beginning to blink on and off.

If you pick up the phone and take Mr. Hata's message first, turn to page 77.

If you hide in the bathroom and wait for Mr. Hata to return, turn to page 79.

There is a long line of people at the Kamigamo Shrine waiting for their New Year's fortunes from Mrs. Hamaguchi. It doesn't seem to bother Takashi or Kenichi a bit. They pass the two-hour wait chatting unconcernedly. Every once in a while they try to assure you of Mrs. Hamaguchi's extraordinary talents.

Finally it's your turn. The three of you are ushered into a small building where Mrs. Hamaguchi receives clients. The air is thick with a heavy, pungent incense. Takashi hands an assistant a ten-thousand-yen note, worth about fifty dollars, and he lifts the red curtain covering the door to the room where Mrs. Hamaguchi sits.

Go on to the next page.

She is surprisingly young and quite friendly. Takashi introduces you and proceeds to relate briefly the events of the morning. As soon as he finishes, Mrs. Hamaguchi reaches over, touches Takashi's arm, and closes her eyes. She sits for several minutes this way, as if she's meditating. Her eyelids begin to flutter slightly, and when they stop, she opens her eyes.

"Takashi, I see several ways of getting the bowl back. There is one way over water and another over land. But the best way for you, I think, is to sit and wait for the bowl to return by itself. The Shino bowl has a strong sense of its own destiny, and it will not fall easily into evil or corrupt hands."

Go on to the next page.

"I see several different people trying to possess the bowl," Mrs. Hamaguchi continues, "but another, stronger spirit is watching over it and protecting it.

"Yes, when the tea bowl, Yukisoo, returns to you, it will be imbued with the power and energy of this guardian. It will be an even more splendid tea utensil than before."

Takashi and Kenichi bow low and thank Mrs. Hamaguchi profusely. You're too surprised by her pronouncement to do much of anything.

When you walk back out of the grounds of the shrine, Takashi asks, "What would you two like to do for the rest of the day? Frankly, my stomach could use a little lunch. It will be on me."

"You mean, you're going to give up looking just like that? Just because Mrs. Hamaguchi says to?" you ask incredulously.

Takashi and Kenichi look at each other in surprise, and then at you. "Of course," Takashi says. "What else is there to do?"

Kenichi puts his arm around your shoulder. "I know this is hard for a Westerner to accept," he says, "but Mrs. Hamaguchi had a very clear reading. I'm sure she was right. Don't worry."

"Come have sushi with us," Takashi says. "It will make the wait pass more pleasantly."

If you decide to go along with Takashi and Kenichi for lunch, turn to page 89.

If you decide that, as long as Takashi and Kenichi feel this way, you can't be of any help and might as well go home, turn to page 95.

Just when you're on the verge of despair, a small marina looms into view. It's a Lake Shore Patrol office! You tie up the boat and burst into the office. A dozing patrolman jerks awake.

"I've just escaped from a Yakuza hideout further up the lake. They've stolen a famous tea bowl from Ura Senke in Kyoto, and they're going to sell it this afternoon. You have to help me get it back!" you gasp to the man on duty.

Immediately he calls all patrolmen in the vicinity to report to his office at once. He also calls down to the main police station in Otsu to notify them of your report. Turning to you, he says, "We've known that there was a Yakuza headquarters on the lake for some time, but we weren't sure where it was. You might help us crack the mystery. Here's a map of the shoreline in either direction for thirty miles. Those small squares are the houses on the lake. Can you pinpoint the general vicinity?"

You study the map for several minutes. In the meantime six more patrolmen arrive in their boats. "Here!" you shout, pointing. "Right here, near those three small islands. I passed them when I wasn't more than five hundred meters out."

The patrolmen crowd around to look where you point. One of them drums his fingers on the desk. All of them are silent. Finally someone says, "That's the summer house of Michio Maruyama, the big industrialist from Tokyo. It's boarded up this time of year. Are you *sure* that this was where you were?"

Turn to page 78.

"Come on!" you say, and you and Kenichi run down the hall after Mr. Hata. Taking a left, you go through a door and down several flights of steps. Finally the stairwell ends. Mr. Hata has led you to the belly of the ship, where the engine is located. You're bound to catch him now.

You step into the engine room. The noise is deafening. Down at the other end of the room you glimpse Mr. Hata disappearing beyond a door. The door is marked:

DANGER!!
DO NOT ENTER
– CERTIFIED SHIP PERSONNEL ONLY –

If you ignore the warning and go inside anyway, turn to page 91.

If you decide to obey the sign and stake out Hata's cabin instead, turn to page 96.

"Hello, Operator," you say, speaking as gruffly as possible. "This is Cabin Number One Eleven. My message light was on," you say.

"Yes, Mr. Hata," she replies. "I'm glad you called. I have an urgent message from a Mrs. Oda. She asked me to repeat it to you exactly."

"Yes," you reply, grabbing a piece of paper and pencil. "Go ahead."

"Mrs. Oda says, 'There has been a sudden change in weather and it no longer looks like snow. Please return to Kyoto immediately.'"

"Is that it?" you ask.

"Yes, that was all," the operator tells you. "If you will be canceling your trip, contact the steward on your deck."

"Thank you," you say, hanging up.

You turn to Kenichi, who's studying the note. "What do you think it means?" you ask. "And why would anyone cancel a trip like this because the weather changed in a city seventy miles away?"

"Well," Kenichi answers, "it might not have to do with weather. Let's just suppose that Mr. Hata *is* carrying the Shino bowl in that box. Or at least he *thinks* he is. The bowl's name, Yukisoo, means 'it looks like snow.' The message says 'it no longer looks like snow.' In Japanese that's the same way you'd say 'it's not Yukisoo.' Maybe the message is trying to tell Hata that he's got the wrong bowl. My guess is that Mr. Hata and Mrs. Oda are in on this together, and something went wrong."

"Kenichi, you're a genius!" you exclaim, slapping your friend on the back.

Turn to page 88.

"Yes," you answer, staring at the map one more time. "Those are the only small islands on this whole map. I'm *sure* that's where I was."

The head officer says, "Well, we'll check out any lead at all. Let's go."

A half hour later you emerge from the thick fog thirty feet from the sandy beach at the edge of Maruyama's property. It's the same house, all right, but something's changed. The windows are shuttered, and the small rowboat in the boathouse has disappeared. You and the patrolmen get out to walk around the house, but there is no sign of life anywhere.

"No one's been here in months," one of the men says. "Sorry, kid."

"But I'm *positive* that this is the place. I took the motorboat from that slip right there!" you say.

"I wouldn't be surprised if you did," the officer tells you gently. "Now you know how hard it is for us to catch the Yakuza. Sometimes they just disappear like smoke."

The End

"Come on," you say to Kenichi. "Let's hide ourselves in the shower. Mr. Hata could return any minute!"

You tuck yourselves out of sight. Ten minutes later you hear Mr. Hata enter the room. He goes straight to the phone and asks for his message. You and Kenichi look at each other and nod in silent agreement. Now is your chance to take him by surprise.

Go on to the next page.

Boom! You kick open the door karate-style, and the two of you leap for Mr. Hata. He is so surprised that he barely resists. Tying him up with sheets, you say, "Okay, Hata. Tell us. What's in the box that's so precious? It's not the tea bowl Yukisoo by any chance?"

"I *thought* it was," Mr. Hata replies, "but that

message just said that the bowl I've got is a fake. We were double-crossed."

"What do you mean, *we*?" you demand.

Go on to the next page.

"Mrs. Oda and myself. Actually she cooked this whole thing up. I was just supposed to deliver it to the buyer in Munich. I borrowed the proper exit stamps needed from the ministry to get the bowl through customs. She's paying me one hundred thousand dollars to deliver it. That's the whole reason I did it. I need the money for my kids' tuition."

You and Kenichi look at each other. You're not sure whether or not to believe Mr. Hata's story.

"Untie me, please," he begs. "I'll help you get the bowl back, I swear. I don't like Mrs. Oda anyway."

If you decide to believe Mr. Hata and untie him, turn to page 86.

If you decide to leave Mr. Hata where he is for now and return to Kyoto with the "fake" bowl, turn to page 90.

Without thinking of the danger you're in, you quickly climb through the window, grab the tea bowl, and climb out again. You can hear voices around at the front, so you head into the woods. Ten minutes later you're climbing over a fence that surrounds the property. As you hop to the ground you hear the barking of an attack dog up the hill coming toward you. Two men follow in the distance.

You scramble up onto the road and run across, almost getting hit by a truck. Up ahead you see a train station. You rush toward it. But you're getting exhausted. Your breath is coming in gasps. . . . You stumble. . . . Someone shouts "Stop that kid!" You look back and see the two men climbing over the fence after you.

A crowded bus slows to a stop alongside you. The driver must think you're trying to catch it. At the same time an express train marked KYOTO steams past you toward the station one hundred yards away.

If you get onto the bus, turn to page 111.

If you make a dash for the train,
turn to page 114.

You take a cab to the Blue Rabbit only to find out that Akiko Tanaka won't be in to work till the next night. "Why don't you talk with Michiko Mori? She's Akiko's best friend," another bar hostess suggests. "I'll go get her."

You slide into one of the plush blue velvet booths to wait. A pretty young woman dressed in a chic light-green kimono comes up and says, "Hi. I'm Michiko. Can I help you?"

"We'd like to ask you some questions about your friend, Akiko Tanaka," you tell her.

"Are you friends of hers?" Michiko asks.

"Of sorts," Takashi answers. "We're from Ura Senke."

"Oh, Akiko just loves that place. She says it makes her feel so peaceful and happy just to *be* there," Michiko replies. "She *needs* the peace these days, I suppose. Last month her grandfather, whom she lives with, became very ill. Then a week ago, her old boyfriend, who's fallen in with the Yakuza, came by. He pestered her and pestered her, but she wouldn't tell me about what. Sometimes I think it's all making her a bit crazy."

"What do you mean by that?" you ask.

Go on to the next page.

"Well, she'll kill me when she knows I've said anything, but last week she asked me to pick up two tea bowls she'd commissioned from an art dealer here in town. They were identical as far as I could tell, and somewhat crude. They were glazed a grayish white—nothing particularly pretty. I would never have spent five hundred thousand yen for them. But then, I don't practice tea, and I don't know about these things."

"Five hundred thousand yen! That's over two thousand dollars!" you say in surprise. "Where could we find Akiko right now?"

"Probably at home," Michiko tells you. "Please don't tell her I told you all this."

"Don't worry," you tell her, standing up to leave. "Come on, you guys," you say to your friends. "My instinct tells me we don't have a moment to lose!"

Turn to page 98.

"He sounds as if he's telling the truth, Kenichi," you say. "What do you think?"

"You're right. Let's untie him," Kenichi answers.

But seconds later you realize you've forgotten one of the main rules of detective work: Never trust anyone. As soon as Mr. Hata is untied, he uses the same sheets to strangle you and Kenichi.

The End

"I've got an idea," you say. "Let's leave Mr. Hata here and let him continue to Germany. He'll discover the mistake eventually, but in the meantime we can go back to Kyoto. Perhaps with the help of the police we can get a confession from Mrs. Oda. The bowl itself shouldn't be far behind."

"What are we waiting for?" Kenichi asks.

You check the hallway, but there's no Mr. Hata in sight. Hurrying off the ship, you leave the dock and hail a cab for Kyoto. Instructing the driver to take you directly to Mrs. Oda's, you tell Kenichi, "We can always get help from the police if we can't shame her into a confession ourselves."

When you arrive at Mrs. Oda's, an old servant informs you that his mistress is out, but he invites you to wait. Three hours later there is still no sign of Mrs. Oda, and it's getting late. You finally ask to use the phone to call Takashi at Ura Senke.

"Where have you *been*?" Takashi asks anxiously. "We were worried sick about you. We found the Shino bowl hours ago!"

Turn to page 109.

"Okay," you say, accepting Takashi's offer. "I guess I could use a little lunch myself."

The three of you eat your fill of raw fish and rice and walk back to Ura Senke afterward. You arrive at the school around dusk. A lustrous blue light bathes the sky, and you can't help noticing how beautiful everything looks when you walk through the garden of the Yu-in tea hut.

Sliding back the rear entrance to the hut, Takashi exclaims in a low voice, "Ah-ha!"

An old wooden box is lying on the floor. Takashi opens it to reveal a misshappen white bowl, large enough to hold in both hands. The bowl looks rather ordinary at first, but when Takashi pulls it out, the white surface absorbs the lovely blue light of dusk.

Takashi hands Yukisoo over, and you cradle the bowl gently, mesmerized. It seems to shimmer as if it were a source of light itself. You can easily pick out the snow clouds on its surface.

You don't know how long you've been staring at it when Kenichi looks at his watch and says, "Oh, my gosh. We're supposed to be at your house for dinner in fifteen minutes! Let's go!"

The End

"You can't trust anyone," you tell Kenichi. "Let's leave him here, where we won't have to worry about him. We'll take the bowl, fake or not, back to Kyoto with us. It may come in handy."

Suddenly there's a loud knock at the door. "Open up, Mr. Hata. This is the police!"

You go to open the door. "Officer, we already have the criminal tied up!" you say.

The door swings open, and four policemen burst past you into the cabin. Convinced that Mr. Hata is securely tied, their chief turns to you. "Good work, kids. Now, where are the pearls?"

Turn to page 115.

You feel for your pocket knife and turn the heavy metal latch to the forbidden room. After all, you don't know how ruthless this Mr. Hata character is.

You step inside a few feet. "There's no one here," you gasp in wonder, staring at the empty space.

"And there's no other exit either," Kenichi adds.

Suddenly the door behind you clicks shut—and someone locks it from the other side. You scream and pound at the door, but no one hears you over the noise of the engine.

It may be days before you're discovered.

The End

With a little effort you manage to shut the padlock on the trap-door latch.

"None of you are going anywhere!" you shout through the door. The men inside curse and shove against the door, but the lock holds. You hop up and rush back up the stairs to the library to call the police.

The bookcase opens with a shove. Out of nowhere two policemen grab you. "We've got one of them!" one bellows. A sea of navy uniforms suddenly surrounds you.

"Wait a minute!" you yell. "I'm not one of them! I was kidnapped!"

Turn to page 53.

94

Akiko Tanaka lives in a small farming village, and you find her house with little difficulty. Takashi knocks at the ancient wooden door. An old woman answers.

"Is Miss Akiko Tanaka in?" Takashi inquires.

"Akiko is with her grandfather at the moment, helping him prepare for tea ceremony," she replies. Seeing the disappointed looks on all your faces, she adds, "But please join us for the tea ceremony, if you would. I know my husband would be honored to have you as guests. Besides, there are only Akiko and myself to attend." She bows deeply, saying again, "It would be a great honor."

Takashi pauses almost imperceptibly before accepting politely. You look at Kenichi questioningly. He whispers, "It would be bad luck to refuse an invitation to tea ceremony on a New Year's day."

The three of you file through the Tanaka residence after the old woman. You notice that it is extremely spare, but immaculate. Its cleanliness makes you feel refreshed. You continue out into a rear garden, where Akiko's grandmother motions you to sit on small woven mats that are spread out on a bench. Looking around, you are reminded of the calm, tranquil atmosphere of the garden at Ura Senke earlier this day.

As Takashi compliments the old woman on her tea garden, Kenichi turns to you. "Have you ever been to a tea ceremony before?" he asks in a low voice. When you shake your head, he adds, "Then just follow me, and do as I do."

Turn to page 101.

"My mother can use me at home," you tell Takashi and Kenichi. "Your family is coming for dinner. You two go on alone."

"Okay," Kenichi answers, smiling. "We'll report on the situation then."

"Right," Takashi agrees. "Thank you for coming, and we'll see you later."

You spend the rest of the afternoon marveling at your friends' total acceptance of Mrs. Hamaguchi's predictions and wondering whether they're a little foolish. But when Takashi and Kenichi arrive with their parents for dinner, they both smile at you knowingly. As soon as the three of you are alone in your room, you ask, "Well, what happened?"

Turn to page 105.

96

You find out that Mr. Hata is staying in First Class Cabin Number 111. The door to the cabin is unlocked, and there are no signs of Mr. Hata inside.

"Let's wait, Kenichi," you suggest. "He's bound to show up sooner or later."

An hour and a half passes without any sign of Mr. Hata. You look at your watch nervously. It's 3:15. The ship is scheduled to depart in fifteen minutes. A voice over the loudspeaker announces: "All persons aboard ship not traveling to Germany, please disembark immediately."

Kenichi turns to you. "I just *know* that Mr. Hata is on this ship someplace. He'll probably show up the minute we leave port. But we don't know for a fact he's got the tea bowl!"

"You're right. I just didn't like the way he ran off when he saw us. He was awfully nervous," you say.

"If we stay and nothing turns up," Kenichi adds brightly, "we can probably get a tugboat ride back into Kobe."

If you decide to stay on board, turn to page 66.

If you decide to head back to Kyoto and follow other leads, turn to page 52.

Mrs. Oda was killed trying to swindle the Shino bowl from this gang of crooks. They drove her car into the lake to get rid of all the evidence. Meanwhile the Shino bowl will be sold on the black market to an Arab in a few days. But you'll never know that. The car sinks to the bottom of the lake, and no one ever finds you.

The End

An hour later you're knocking at Akiko's front door. It's now late afternoon.

"Is Akiko in?" you ask the old woman who answers the door. She disappears inside the house and returns, saying, "Akiko will see you in the dining room. Follow me."

The old woman pulls back a white paper screen. A young woman inside, who, you think, must be Akiko, is kneeling on a mat at a low red table, staring at a wooden box in front of her.

"Thank you, Grandma," Akiko says to the old woman before she leaves. Looking at the three of you, she adds, "Please sit down."

She pushes the wooden box across the table toward Takashi. "I believe you are looking for this. I was going to return it this afternoon. It's the missing tea bowl."

Before Takashi can say anything, she says, "I took it so my grandfather could use it for his New Year's tea ceremony. He is old and poor, but a great follower of tea." Almost in a whisper she adds, "He is also dying. I thought it would be appropriate if he could use this masterpiece for his last New Year's ceremony."

Turn to page 106.

You direct your driver to Mrs. Oda's. By the time your cab pulls up to her front gate, it's dark outside. A servant answers the ring and says, "Mrs. Oda is out, but another guest is waiting for her to return as well. Why don't you join him?"

As you follow the old man inside you wonder if the other guest is Takashi. You and Kenichi both gasp in shock when the door to the parlor is opened. Mr. Hata is sitting there!

Getting over his own surprise, he asks irritably, "What are you two doing here?"

"We're here for the same reason as you—the missing tea bowl," you tell him boldly.

"You work for Mrs. Oda too?" he asks suspiciously. "She never said anything about anyone else."

"Isn't that her way?" Kenichi says, playing along. "She keeps us all a secret from one other."

"Probably wise," Mr. Hata comments. "But now that we know about one other, I suppose it's okay to talk."

Turn to page 107.

A little while later, an old, stooped man walks down the stone path from the tea hut in the far corner of the garden. A young woman, who must be Akiko, walks next to him, carrying a bucket of water. They stop at a stone basin where the old man sprinkles water on the ground. Rinsing his mouth and washing his hands, he pours the rest of the water into the basin. He turns toward the waiting bench. Takashi, Kenichi, and the old woman stand, so you do too. Takashi takes one step forward. He and the old man bow silently to each other. Your host turns around, takes his granddaughter's arm, and heads back into the tea house.

One by one you follow, first stopping to wash your hands at the stone basin and rinse your mouth. Everyone is silent. You're itching to ask questions, but you decide to give yourself over to the calm of the moment and enjoy the unfolding scene. You follow Kenichi inside the low door to the tea hut, carefully removing your shoes as he does.

The room is simpler than the tea hut at Ura Senke. A single camellia bud peers out of a bamboo vase hanging to one side of the alcove. Next to it is a scroll with the poem:

> *The New Year's flake falls into*
> *   the rice paddy and melts.*
> *Life is like snow—*
> *It disappears!*

Turn to page 103.

As soon as the old woman, who was last, shuts the guest's entrance with a decisive click, Akiko enters through another door. She carries a small charcoal brazier and an old iron kettle. Setting them down, she arranges the charcoal carefully and places the kettle over the coals. In a moment the kettle begins to sing—a haunting, melancholy sound, not unlike wind in the trees.

As if it's his cue, the old man opens the door, carrying a—a white mottled tea bowl with a tea whisk resting inside! As he sets the bowl down beside the brazier, you can see the gray splotches on one side. It's the missing Shino piece! You're sure of it.

You glance over at Takashi, but he wears an expression of intense concentration. Hasn't he noticed? You look at Kenichi, who wears a similar mask. Maybe it *isn't* the bowl? But you look at the bowl again as the old man scoops the powdered green tea into it and pours hot water over the powder. It *has* to be the one.

If you decide to break the silence and ask the old man if you're right, turn to page 110.

If you decide to let Takashi ask about the bowl, go on to the next page.

104

Takashi says nothing when the old man offers him the frothy green tea. He sips from the tea bowl and hands it back. The old man carefully cleans the lip before offering the tea to Kenichi, then to you. The tea, though bitter, is warm and pleasant. You are struck by the calm, clean quiet, the old man's slow movements, the distant hiss of wind in the pine trees.

After he has served his wife and granddaughter, the old man washes and wipes the bowl. Takashi asks if he may inspect it. Now he will say something, you think, but he merely hands the tea bowl back to the old man after examining it. Bowing deeply, Takashi says, "Rarely have I been the guest at such a fine tea ceremony. Would you be so kind as to sign Yukisoo's box?"

"It will be an honor to accept such a request," the man replies.

Akiko fetches the box from the preparation area and holds it while her grandfather signs his name alongside the three others already on the lid. Gently placing the tea bowl inside, he passes the box to Takashi and bows low. Takashi thanks the old man, adding, "There is no need for you to see us out." The old man disappears behind the door by which he entered. Takashi stands to leave. When you follow, you notice tears of happiness streaming down the face of Akiko's grandmother. As you head back through the garden, the door to the tea hut reopens. The old man exchanges a last bow with Takashi before shutting the door with a click.

Turn to page 108.

"The bowl showed up, just as Mrs. Hamaguchi predicted," Takashi tells you.

"We had lunch and walked back to the tearoom at about dusk, and there it was. Someone had put it just inside the door to the utensil room of the tea hut," Kenichi adds.

You stare at both your friends, wide-eyed and speechless. "So the fortune-teller was right!" you finally blurt out.

"Yup." Kenichi nods as proudly as if he'd made the prediction himself. Poking you in the ribs, he adds, jokingly, "Maybe Mrs. Hamaguchi can tell us how we're going to do in math this semester!"

The End

All three of you are silent. This young woman's honesty and integrity are a turn of events you weren't expecting. Finally you ask, "But why the two look-alikes, then?"

Akiko's eyebrows raise in horror. "Who told you? Michiko?"

"It doesn't make any difference. I just want to understand the whole puzzle," you tell her.

In a shaky voice Akiko tells you her story. "Three weeks ago Mrs. Oda approached me and asked if I would steal the Shino bowl for her and substitute a fake that she had had made. Under normal circumstances I would have refused outright, but she offered me five million yen—almost twenty-five thousand dollars—to do it. My grandfather has no medical insurance, so I agreed.

"Then, last week, a former friend of mine, who had somehow heard about Mrs. Oda's plan, asked me to make yet another substitute. This second offer gave me a chance. I gave fakes to both of them and kept the original bowl to use and then return. It would have violated the whole spirit of tea to have such a bowl fall into the hands of either group."

Takashi bows very low, saying, "I admire your courage, and I thank you on behalf of Ura Senke and all its masters and students. We are indebted to you forever."

The End

"Sure," you agree, trying to sound casual. "Why aren't you on your way to Germany anyway?"

"Mrs. Oda left a message in my cabin to return to Kyoto immediately because I had the wrong bowl. Take a look at this," he adds, reaching into a box at his side. "Someone substituted a fake somewhere along the line. Not that the moron in Germany who wants to buy it could tell the difference," he adds, chuckling.

You take the splotchy rough white bowl from his hands, laughing along with him.

"Where's Mrs. Oda now?" Kenichi asks offhandedly.

"Off getting the original bowl back, according to her servant," he replies.

"Excuse me," you interrupt, "but I have to use the bathroom. I'll be right back."

Kenichi and Mr. Hata continue to talk as you close the door and pad quietly up the hall to a phone. You dial a number and wait for a second until someone answers.

"Hello, police? I'd like to report the theft of a National Treasure, a tea bowl owned by Ura Senke. If you come to the following address within half an hour, you can catch the criminals, and probably recover the bowl. . . ."

The End

As soon as the three of you are on your way back to Ura Senke with Yukisoo, you ask, "Takashi, why didn't you ask Akiko why she took the bowl?"

"Some things are better left unsaid, better left unknown. This was one of them," Takashi answers.

His reply does not satisfy you. "Well, then tell me why you asked her grandfather to sign the box?"

Kenichi turns to you. "The old man had the true spirit of tea. His name will now be immortalized in tea history with the three other great masters who have signed Yukisoo's lid."

"The 'true spirit of tea'? What's that?" you press your friend.

"You will have to study the way of tea to find out."

The End

"What? You *found*

"Yes," Takashi say
teacher and I were tal
the school office wher
to the tea hut to chec
was in its box on the
area. It hadn't been the
one must have return

"We have a good

"Have the detectives wait, and we'll come right
over to tell our story."

A half hour later you are sitting in the Ura Senke
office with everyone else and describing your trip
to Kobe. The chief investigator agrees with your
theory. "It does seem to point to Oda and Hata as
the masterminds behind all this, even if the bowl
has been safely returned. We'll call her in for questioning first thing in the morning," he assures you.

But the questioning never takes place. The next
day Mrs. Oda's body floats to shore at Lake Biwa,
riddled with bullet holes. A year later the police are
still unable to make any connection between her
death and the theft of the Shino bowl. The mystery
of Ura Senke remains a mystery.

The End

The old ma
of frothy, bri
me, sir, b
called

...n is about to serve Takashi the bowl ...lliant green tea when you say, "Excuse ...ut isn't that the famous Shino tea bowl ...Yukisoo?"

...kiko jerks involuntarily, and Takashi and Kenchi look at you in shock. There is a glint of anger in Takashi's eyes. The old woman stares at the floor in embarrassed silence. The old man ignores them all, however. "Yes, and a magnificent bowl it is. Auspicious for a New Year's tea, I think," he says calmly.

The tea ceremony proceeds, the old man serving each one of you. But the spell is broken. The mood inside the room becomes uncomfortable and awkward. Finally, when the old man has finished serving Akiko, he cleans the tea bowl carefully, methodically, and hands it over to Takashi, saying, "I thank you for the generous loan of the Shino bowl."

Takashi looks at the bowl for a moment before handing it back to the old man. "Please keep it a while longer; it will benefit in the hands of such a master," he says.

Later, Kenichi tells you that such a gesture was the only way Takashi could atone for your rude question. You know where the bowl is, and that one day it will be safely returned, but you will never quite be able to forgive yourself for ruining a lovely tea ceremony.

The End

The open bus door is directly in front of you. Panting, you climb on. The two men run after the bus, yelling and waving their arms wildly, but no one notices. Most of the people standing near you are staring at the tea bowl in your hands. You look at it carefully for the first time yourself. It is slightly irregular in shape with a mottled white glaze. There are grayish splotches near the lip on one side that do look like snow clouds, if you squint a bit.

Oh, no, you think. What if someone recognizes the bowl? But a quick look around tells you that the crowd's attention has shifted to something going on up ahead. Looking out, you can see a New Year's festival in full swing, and the bus is pulling up to let riders off. You try to get out of the way, but the bus is too crowded. People are already moving toward the door.

Go on to the next page.

The door swings open, and the crowd pushes you out onto the street. You trip on the curb—and the Shino bowl flies through the air. It hits the pavement with a crash, splintering into countless pieces.

The crowd rushes past without even glancing down, on its way to celebrate the New Year.

The End

114

Ignoring the bus, you make a dash for the station. The two men in pursuit have practically caught up with you when you leap onto the train a split second before the doors slide shut. They bang on the windows, but the conductor ignores them and the train lurches forward.

An hour later you are standing in front of Ura Senke's gate. You hurry toward the Yu-in Tearoom and are relieved to see both your friends, as well as several older Japanese men. Takashi is giving information to a police officer.

"Takashi! Kenichi! Look! I got the bowl. Some crooks at a farmhouse on Lake Biwa had it," you exclaim.

Your friends jump up, smiling, while one of the older men reaches gently for the bowl to examine it.

Kenichi asks, "How did you get it?"

Turn to page 116.

"Pearls?" you ask incredulously. "What pearls?"

"The strand of perfect ten-millimeter pearls that Mr. Hata is trying to smuggle out of the country for his friend Mrs. Oda," the officer answers.

"Here they are," says one of the other policemen as he breaks open the top to the wooden box Hata was carrying. "Imbedded in the wood. Nice try, Hata." He chuckles.

"But we were looking for a stolen tea bowl—a National Treasure!" you tell the officer.

"What? This?" the officer asks, picking up the tea bowl that has rolled out of the box onto the bed. "Come on, kids, don't be modest. This bowl is nice, but it's no National Treasure. You knew about the pearls. Who tipped you off?"

You try to tell the officers you had no idea about the stolen pearls, but they refuse to believe you. In a short while some press photographers show up.

Tomorrow your pictures will be plastered across the front page of every newspaper in Japan as the heroes of a crime you didn't even solve.

The End

"Mrs. Oda went to this fancy old farmhouse and got out of the car. As soon as it was quiet I got out of the car and started circling the house. I heard voices coming from a room and went to listen. But before I could hear anything, two shots were fired. I think Mrs. Oda was killed, but I sure didn't stay around to find out. In the confusion I just grabbed the bowl and escaped."

"I am afraid your friend was endangered unnecessarily," the man examining the bowl interjects. "This bowl is a fake."

"What?" Takashi asks.

"A fake. A good copy, but not the real thing," the man tells Takashi patiently.

"What do we do now?" Kenichi asks in despair. "Start again at the beginning?"

"At least with Mrs. Oda dead, there's one less suspect," you say cheerfully.

The End

ABOUT THE AUTHOR

SHANNON GILLIGAN graduated from Williams College in 1981. While a student, she spent a year studying at Doshisha University in Kyoto, Japan. Ms. Gilligan is also the author of *The Search for Champ, The Three Wishes,* and *Mona Is Missing* in the Bantam Skylark Choose Your Own Adventure series. When she's not traveling to do research for her books, she lives in Warren, Vermont.

ABOUT THE ILLUSTRATOR

PAUL ABRAMS has worked as an artist for Marvel Comics and *Heavy Metal* magazine. He has also taught art professionally and was a rock musician for several years. In the Bantam Choose Your Own Adventure series, he has illustrated *War With the Evil Power Master* and *The Dragons' Den.* Mr. Abrams lives in New Paltz, New York.

CHOOSE YOUR OWN ADVENTURE ®

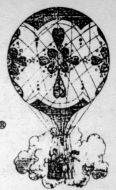

"You'll want all the books in the exciting Choose Your Own Adventure series. Each book takes you through dozens of fantasy adventures—under the sea, in a space colony, into the past—in which *you* are the main character. What happens next in the story depends on the choices *you* make, and *only you* can decide how the story ends!"

Make sure you have all these great Interplanetary Spy books!